RABBIT'S WISH

WORDS BY PAUL STEWART
PICTURES BY CHRIS RIDDELL

A

ANDERSEN PRESS

LONDON

"Look at the sky, Hedgehog," said Rabbit.
"It's all beautiful and red."
"I like it better when it's twinkly and black,"
said Hedgehog. "Besides, you know what they say
about red skies."
"Remind me," said Rabbit.
"Red sky in the morning, shepherd's warning,"
said Hedgehog. "Rain is on its way."

Hedgehog yawned. "Time for me to go to bed," he said.
"So soon?" said Rabbit.
"Yes, Rabbit," said Hedgehog. "You are a day creature
and I am a night creature. That is the way it is."
Rabbit nodded sadly. "Night-night, Hedgehog.
I mean, *day-day!*"

As Hedgehog disappeared from view,
Rabbit sighed a great big, lonely sigh.
"I wish," he said, "that just for once,
Hedgehog could stay up all day with me."

With his friend gone, Rabbit did what he always
did. He had breakfast.

A little grass.

A dandelion leaf . . .

Suddenly – *plop* – a raindrop
landed on his nose.

"Bother!" said Rabbit. "Hedgehog was right. Rain was on its way. And now it's here!"

As Rabbit hopped back to his burrow, the rain grew heavier and heavier. "How wet it is!" he said.

Rabbit shook the water from his fur,
wiped the mud from his paws,
and scampered underground.

"My burrow," said Rabbit happily. "So warm.
So cosy. So *dry!*" He frowned. "But it is also rather
messy," he said. "As it is raining *out*side, I will stay
*in*side and tidy up."

Rabbit busied himself all morning.

He swept the floor.

He made his bed.

He sorted through his treasures, one by one . . .

The ball.   The string.   The woolly thing.

And most precious of all, the bottle of moonlight that Hedgehog had given him.

"Oh, Hedgehog, I *do* miss you," said Rabbit. "I . . ."

"Water!" Rabbit cried. "There's water in my burrow!"
The water was trickling down the tunnel and seeping up through the floor. It quickly soaked Rabbit's bed of straw, and set his treasures bobbing.

With the bottle of moonlight in one arm, and the ball, the string and the woolly thing in the other,
Rabbit hurried from his burrow.

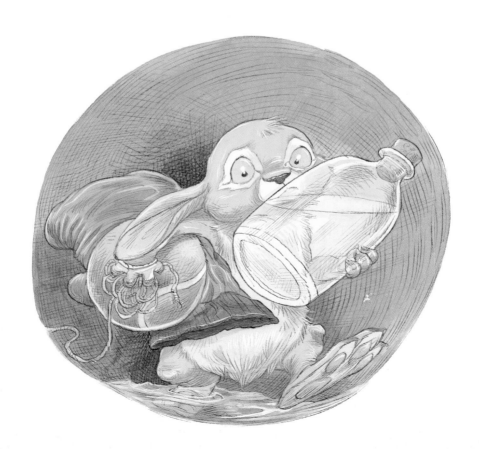

RABBIT couldn't believe his eyes.
The rain was heavier than ever.
And the lake! It was higher than he had seen it before —
so high that Rabbit's little hill had been turned into an island.

Far away, on the other side of the lake, the tops of Hedgehog's
bramble patch poked up above the swirling, muddy water.
Rabbit dropped his treasures. He ran this way and that.
"Hedgehog!" he cried. "Hedgehog, where are you?"

"Here I am," said a little voice.
Rabbit spun round. Hedgehog was standing down by
the water's edge.

"Hedgehog!" cried Rabbit.
"Rabbit!" cried Hedgehog.

"I was so *worried!*" said Rabbit.
"There was no need to be worried," said Hedgehog.
"I'm a good swimmer. When the water woke me,
I was worried about *you!* So I swam across the lake
to find you."

Rabbit stared at his friend with wide-open eyes.
"You're so brave!" he said. "But you mustn't catch cold."
He put the woolly thing on Hedgehog's head.

"But what are we going to do *now*, Hedgehog?" said Rabbit.
"My burrow is full of water. Your bed is at the bottom
of the lake. And it's *still* raining!"
"I know just what we can do," said Hedgehog. "We can play."
"Yes!" said Rabbit. "We can play together in the rain!"

They played catch.

They played tug-of-war.

They played boats.

The rain stopped, the sky cleared and the stars came out.
Rabbit and Hedgehog sat down at the edge of the lake.
"Hedgehog," said Rabbit. "I have a confession."
"What do you mean?" said Hedgehog.
"I have something to tell you," said Rabbit . . .

"It was my fault that everything happened.
I wished that you could stay up all day with me."
He looked down sorrowfully. "And my wish came true."
"I'm glad that it did," said Hedgehog. "Maybe next time
I will wish that you could stay up all night. With me!"
"I'd like that," said Rabbit. He yawned. "But now it's time
for *me* to go to bed."

"Night-night, Rabbit," said Hedgehog.
"Night-night, Hedgehog," said Rabbit.